melville house classics

THE
LEMOINE
AFFAIR

THE LEMOINE AFFAIR

MARCEL PROUST

TRANSLATED BY CHARLOTTE MANDELL

 MELVILLE HOUSE PUBLISHING
BROOKLYN, NEW YORK

THE LEMOINE AFFAIR WAS FIRST PUBLISHED IN *LE FIGARO* IN
JANUARY, 1904 AND FEBRUARY-MARCH, 1908. THEY WERE
SUBSEQUENTLY REVISED AND COLLECTED IN THE BOOK
PASTICHES ET MÉLANGES (GALLIMARD) IN 1918.

TRANSLATION © CHARLOTTE MANDELL 2008

SERIES DESIGN: DAVID KONOPKA

MELVILLE HOUSE PUBLISHING
145 PLYMOUTH STREET
BROOKLYN, NY 11201

WWW.MHPBOOKS.COM

ISBN 978-1-933633-41-1

FIRST MELVILLE HOUSE PRINTING: MAY 2008

LIBRARY OF CONGRESS CATALOGING-IN-PUBLICATION DATA

PROUST, MARCEL, 1871-1922.
  [PASTICHES ET MÉLANGES. ENGLISH]
  THE LEMOINE AFFAIR / MARCEL PROUST ; TRANSLATED BY
CHARLOTTE MANDELL.
    P. CM.
  ISBN 978-1-933633-41-1
  I. MANDELL, CHARLOTTE. II. TITLE.
  PQ2631.R63P313 2008
  843.912--DC22

                                        2008009204

PRINTED IN CANADA.

THE LEMOINE AFFAIR

TABLE OF CONTENTS

The reader may have forgotten, since ten years have now passed, that Lemoine, having falsely claimed to have discovered the secret of making diamonds and having received, because of this claim, more than a million francs from the President of De Beers, Sir Julius Werner, who then brought action against him, was afterwards condemned on July 6, 1909 to six years in prison. This legal affair, which, although insignificant, enthralled public opinion at the time, was selected one evening by me, entirely by chance, as the common theme for a few short pieces in which I would set out to imitate the style of a certain number of writers. Even though offering even the slighest explanation of one's pastiches risks diminishing their effect, nonetheless, lest one's own legitimate self-esteem be ruffled, I might remind the reader that it is the pastiched writer who is imagined as speaking, faithful not only to his particular mind, but also to the language of his time. In the piece by Saint-Simon for example, the words "good man, *bonhomme*" and "good woman" do not at all have the familiar, condescending slant they have today. In his *Memoirs*, Saint-Simon throughout says "good man Chaulnes" (*le bonhomme Chaulnes*) for the Duc de Chaulnes, for whom he had infinite respect, and likewise for many others.

—Marcel Proust

I FROM A NOVEL BY BALZAC

In one of the last months of the year 1907, at one of those "routs" of the Marquise d'Espard thronged with the elite of Parisian aristocracy (the most elegant in Europe, according to M. de Talleyrand, that Roger Bacon of the social organism, who was both a bishop and Prince of Benevento), de Marsay and Rastignac, Comte Félix de Vandenesse, the Ducs de Rhétoré and Grandlieu, Comte Adam Laginski, Maître Octave de Camps, and Lord Dudley, formed a circle around Mme the Princesse de Cadignan, yet without arousing the jealousy of the Marquise. Isn't it in fact one of the greatnesses of the mistress of the house—that Carmelite of worldly success—that she must sacrifice her coquetry, her pride, her very love, to the necessity of creating a salon in which her rivals will at times be the most striking ornament? Isn't she in that respect equivalent to a saint? Doesn't she deserve her share, so dearly acquired, in the social paradise? The Marquise—a young lady from Blamont-Chauvry, related to the Navarreins, the Lenoncourts, and the Chaulieus—held out to each newcomer the hand that Desplein, the greatest scholar of our time (without excepting Claude Bernard) who had been the student of Lavater, declared was the most profoundly mapped he had ever been given to examine. All of a sudden the door opened to the illustrious novelist Daniel d'Arthez. A physicist of the moral world who possessed the genius of both Lavoisier and Bichat—the creator of organic chemistry—would alone be capable of isolating the elements that compose the special sonority of the footsteps of superior men. Hearing those of d'Arthez resound you would have trembled. Only a sublime genius or a great criminal could have walked thus. But isn't genius a kind of crime against the routine of the past that our time punishes more severely than crime itself, since scholars die in hospitals bleaker than any prison?

Athénaïs did not feel any joy at seeing return to her home the lover she hoped to snatch away from her best friend. Thus she pressed the hand of the Princess while preserving the impenetrable calm that women of high society possess at the very instant they are burying a dagger in your heart.

"I am happy for you, my dear friend, that Monsieur d'Arthez has come," she said to Mme de Cadignan, "all the more so since he will be completely surprised; he did not know you would be here."

"He probably thought he would meet Monsieur de Rubempré here, whose talent he admires," Diane replied with an affectionate pout that hid the most biting raillery, since everyone knew that Mme d'Espard did not forgive Lucien for having abandoned her.

"Oh! my angel," the Marquise replied with a surprising ease, "we cannot stop people like that, Lucien will undergo the fate of little d'Esgrignon," she added, confounding all those present by the infamy of these words, each one of which was an overwhelming taunt for the Princess. (See *The Cabinet of Antiquities*.)

"You are speaking of Monsieur de Rubempré," the Vicomtesse de Beauséant said, who had not reappeared in society since the death of M. de Nueil and who, out of a habit peculiar to people who have lived in the country for a long time, eagerly looked forward to surprising Parisians with a piece of news she had just learned. "You know that he is engaged to Clotilde de Grandlieu."

Everyone made a sign to the Vicomtesse to be quiet, since this marriage was still unknown to Mme de Sérizy, whom it would cast into despair.

"People say it's true, but it might not be," the Vicomtesse continued who, without precisely understanding what sort of gaffe she had committed, regretted she had been so demonstrative.

"What you say does not astonish me," she added, "for I was surprised that Clotilde was in love with someone so unattractive."

"But on the contrary, no one is of your opinion, Claire," the Princess cried out, pointing out the Comtesse de Sérizy who was listening.

These words were all the more lost on the Vicomtesse since she was completely unaware of the relationship between Mme de Sérizy and Lucien.

"Unattractive," she tried to correct herself, "unattractive . . . at least for a *young* woman!"

"Picture it to yourself," d'Arthez cried out before he had even given his coat to Paddy, the famous tiger to the late Beaudenord (see *The Secrets of the Princesse de Cadignan*), who was standing in front of him with that immobility which was the specialty of the domestic staffs of the Faubourg Saint-Germain, "yes, just picture it," the great man repeated with that enthusiasm of thinkers that seems ridiculous amidst the profound dissimulation of high society.

"What is it? What should we picture to ourselves," de Marsay asked ironically, giving Félix de Vandenesse and Prince Galathione that ambiguous look, a veritable privilege of those who had lived for a long time in intimacy with MADAME.

"Alvays goot!" the Baron de Nucingen gushed with the frightful vulgarity of parvenus who think that with the help of the coarsest sayings they can put on airs and mimic people like Maxime de Trailles or de Marsay; "unt you haf a goot hott; you are de true brotéctor of de boor, in de Deppities."

(The famous financier had special reasons to bear a grudge against d'Arthez who hadn't given him enough support, when Esther's former lover had sought in vain to have his wife, née Goriot, admitted to the home of Diane de Maufrigneuse).

"Kvik, kvik, sire, mein happiness vill be complete if you find me vorthy of knowing egzakly vat it is I should himagine?"

"Nothing," d'Arthez replied appropriately, "I am speaking to the Marquise."

That was said in such a perfidiously epigrammatic tone that Paul Morand, one of our more impertinent embassy secretaries, murmured, "He is stronger than we!" The Baron, sensing he had been trifled with, felt his blood run cold. Mme Firmiani sweated in her slippers, masterpieces of Polish industry. D'Arthez pretended he didn't notice the comedy that had just played out, of a kind that only Parisian life can offer so profoundly (which explains why the provinces have always provided France with so few men of State) and without pausing at the beautiful Négrepelisse, turning toward Mme de Sérizy with that terrifying sang-froid that can triumph over the greatest obstacles (and for lofty souls are there any like those of the heart?):

"Madame, they have just discovered the secret of making diamonds."

"Dis bizness is eine grreat dreasure," the Baron exclaimed, dazzled.

"But I thought they always made them," Léontine naively replied.

Mme de Cadignan, as a woman of taste, took care not to say a word, whereas bourgeois ladies would have launched into a conversation where they would have inanely flaunted their knowledge of chemistry. But Mme de Sérizy had still not finished that phrase that revealed an incredible ignorance, when Diane, lavishing her whole attention on the Countess, assumed a sublime look. Only Raphael might have been capable of painting it. And indeed, if he had succeeded, he would have given us a counterpart to his famous *Fornarina*, the most prominent of his canvases, the only one that places him above Andrea del Sarto in the esteem of connoisseurs.

To understand the drama that is about to unfold, and to which the scene we have just related may serve as prologue, a few words of explanation are necessary. At the end of the year 1905, a fearful tension reigned in the relationships between France and Germany. Either because Wilhelm II was actually planning to declare war on France, or because he just wanted to give that impression in order to break our alliance with England, the German ambassador received the order to announce to the French government that he was going to present his letters of recall. The kings of finance speculated then on a drop in the market, coming on news of an imminent mobilization. Considerable sums were lost in the stock exchange. For one whole day they sold government bonds that the banker Nucingen, secretly alerted by his friend the minister de Marsay of the resignation of the chancellor Delcassé, which people in Paris didn't hear about until around four o'clock, bought back at a ludicrous price and has kept ever since.

Even Raoul Nathan believed in the war, although Florine's lover, because du Tillet, whose sister-in-law he had wanted to seduce (see *A Daughter of Eve*), had given him a bad steer on the stock market, advocated peace at any price in his newspaper.

France was saved from a disastrous war then only by the intervention, of which for a long time historians have been unaware, of the Maréchal de Montcornet, the strongest man of his century after Napoleon. Even Napoleon was unable to execute his plan of landing in England, the master idea of his reign. Napoleon, Montcornet—isn't there a kind of mysterious resemblance between these two names? I should be careful not to say that they are linked to each other by some occult bond. Perhaps our era, after having doubted all great things without trying to understand them, will be forced to return to the pre-established harmony of Leibniz. What's more, the man who was then at the head of the most colossal diamond business in England was named Werner, Julius Werner—Werner! Doesn't this name seem to you strangely to evoke the Middle Ages? Just hearing it, don't you already see Dr. Faust, bending over his crucibles, with or without Marguerite? Doesn't it imply the idea of the philosopher's stone? Werner! Julius! Werner! Change two letters and you have Werther. *Werther* is by Goethe.

Julius Werner used Lemoine, one of those extraordinary men who, if they are guided by a favorable fate, will be called Geoffrey Saint-Hilaire, Cuvier, Ivan the Terrible, Peter the Great, Charlemagne, Berthollet,

Spalanzani, Volta. Change the circumstances and they will end up like the Maréchal d'Ancre, Balthazar Cleas, Pugachev, Le Tasse, the Comtesse de la Motte or Vautrin. In France, the patent the government grants inventors has no value of its own. That is where we should seek the cause that is paralyzing the whole vast industrial enterprise in our country. Before the Revolution, the Séchards, giants of printing, still used wooden presses in Angoulême, and the Cointet brothers hesitated to buy the second printing patent. (See *Lost Illusions*.) In fact, few people understood the answer Lemoine made to the policemen who had come to arrest him. "What? Would Europe abandon me?" the false inventor had exclaimed with profound terror. The remark bandied about that evening in the salons of the government minister Rastignac passed unnoticed.

"Has that man gone mad?" the Comte de Granville said, surprised.

The former clerk of the attorney Bordin was supposed to take the stand in this case in the name of the public prosecutor's department, having recently recovered, through the marriage of his second daughter to the banker du Tillet, the favorable consideration from the new government that his alliance with the Vandenesses had made him lose, etc.

II   THE "LEMOINE AFFAIR"
BY GUSTAVE FLAUBERT

The heat had become stifling, a bell chimed, some turtledoves took flight, and, the windows having been closed by order of the presiding magistrate, a smell of dust spread. He was old, with a clown's face, wore a gown too narrow for his girth, and had pretensions to wit; his twin sideburns, which a trace of tobacco stained, gave something ornamental and vulgar to his entire person. Since the adjournment of the hearing was prolonged, private exchanges started up; to enter into conversation, the irritable ones complained out loud about the lack of air, and, when someone said he had recognized the Minister of the Interior as the gentleman who was going out, a reactionary sighed, "Poor France!" Taking an orange out of his pocket, a black man won esteem, and, out of a desire for popularity, offered segments of it on a newspaper to his neighbors, excusing himself: first to a clergyman, who stated "he had never eaten anything so good; it is an excellent, refreshing fruit"; but a dowager lady took on an offended air, forbade her daughters to accept anything "from someone they didn't know," while other people, not knowing if the newspaper would get to them, sought to strike up an attitude: several took out their watches, a lady took off her hat. A parrot was mounted on it. Two young men were startled, would much have liked to discover if the bird had been placed there as a souvenir or perhaps out of some sort of eccentric taste. Already the wags were beginning to call out to each other from one bench to the other, and the women, looking at their husbands, were smothering their laughter in their handkerchiefs, when silence was restored, the presiding magistrate seemed to be absorbed in sleeping, and Werner's lawyer began to utter his speech for the plaintiff. He started out with an emphatic tone, spoke for two hours, seemed dyspeptic, and every time he said "Your Honor" collapsed into such a profound bow that you would have thought he was a young woman in front of a king, or a deacon leaving the altar. He was savage about Lemoine, but the elegance of the phrases softened the harshness of the indictment. And his sentences followed each other uninterruptedly, like the gush of a waterfall, like a ribbon unfurling. At times, the monotony of his speech was such that it could no longer be distinguished from silence, like a bell whose vibration persists, like an echo becoming fainter. To conclude, he called to witness the portraits of Presidents Grévy and Carnot, placed above the court; and everyone, raising his head, observed that mildew had overtaken them in this official, unclean room that exhibited our glories and smelled musty. A wide opening divided it down the middle, benches were lined up to the foot of the dais; there was dust on the floor, spiders in the corners of the ceiling, a rat in every hole, and it had to be aired out often because of the closeness of the stove, which was sometimes even more foul-smelling. Lemoine's counsel was brief in his reply. But he had a southern accent, appealed to generous passions, kept taking off his pince-nez. Listening to him, Nathalie felt that confusion to which eloquence leads; a sweetness filled her and her heart heaving, the cambric of her corsage fluttered, like a blade of grass by the edge of a fountain ready to well up, like the plumage of a pigeon about to fly away. Finally the magistrate made a sign, a murmuring rose up, two umbrellas fell down: they were going to hear the defendant once again. All of a sudden the angry gestures of the crowd pointed him out; why hadn't he told the truth, and made the diamond, and patented his invention? Everyone, even the poorest, could have—this was certain—made millions from it. They could even see the money in front of them, with that violence of regret when you think you possess what you mourn. And many abandoned themselves all over again to the loveliness of the dreams they had fashioned, when upon news of the discovery they had glimpsed the fortune, before being foiled by the swindle.

For some, it had meant retiring from business, having a mansion on the Avenue du Bois, influence at the Academy; and even a yacht that would have taken them in the summer to cold countries—but not to the Pole, which is not without interest, but the food there smells of oil, the twenty-four-hour day must bother your sleep, and also how do you keep clear of the polar bears?

For some, millions were not enough; they would have played them all at once on the stock market; and, buying shares at the lowest rate the day before they rose back up—a friend would have let them know when— they could see their capital increase a hundredfold in a few hours. Rich as Carnegie then, though they would take care not to waste it on humanitarian utopias. (In any case, what's the use? A billion shared among all the French wouldn't make one single person rich, it's been calculated.) But, leaving luxury to the vain, they would only seek comfort and influence, would have themselves elected President of the Republic, Ambassador to Constantinople, would have their bedrooms padded with cork that would deaden the sound of their neighbors. They would not join the Jockey Club, having the correct opinion of the aristocracy. A patent of nobility from the Pope attracted them more. Perhaps you could have a papal title without paying. But then what would be the good of so many millions? In short, they would augment the annual gift to the Pope while still blaming the Church. What possible use can the Pope have for five million pieces of lacework, while so many country priests are dying of hunger?

But some, thinking of the wealth that could have come to them, felt ready to faint; for they would have placed it all at the feet of a woman by whom they had been scorned until now, who would have finally given them the secret of her kiss and the sweetness of her body. They saw themselves with her, in the country, till the end of their days, in a house all made of whitewood, by the dark shore of a large river. They would have known the cry of the petrel, the coming of the fog, the rocking of the ships, the formation of clouds, and would have remained for hours with her body on their lap, watching the tide rise and the moorings knock together from their terrace, in a wicker chair, beneath a blue-striped marquee, on the bowling green. And they ended up seeing nothing more than two clusters of purple flowers, trailing down to the swift water that they can almost touch, in the bleak light of an afternoon without sun, along a reddish wall crumbling away. For those people, the very excess of their distress took away the strength to curse the accused; but everyone hated him, reflecting that he had cheated them of debauchery, of honors, of fame, of genius; sometimes of more indefinable fancies, of all that was profound and sweet that everyone harbored, ever since childhood, each in the particular folly of his dream.

III   CRITIQUE OF THE NOVEL BY M. GUSTAVE FLAUBERT ON "THE LEMOINE AFFAIR," BY SAINTE-BEUVE, IN HIS COLUMN IN *THE CONSTITUTIONAL*

The Lemoine Affair . . . by Mr. Gustave Flaubert! Especially so soon after *Salammbô*, the title is altogether a surprising one. What's this? The author has set up his easel in the midst of Paris, at the law courts in the Palais de Justice, in the very chamber of criminal appeals . . . : and here we thought he was still in Carthage! Mr. Flaubert—estimable both in his impulse and his predilection—is not one of those writers whom Martial so subtly mocked and who, past masters in one field, or with the reputation of being so, confine themselves to it, dig themselves down into it, anxious above all not to offer any foothold for criticism, exposing only one wing at a time in any maneuver. Mr. Flaubert, on the contrary, likes to multiply his reconnaissance missions and his sorties, and confront the enemy on all sides—nay, he accepts all challenges, regardless of the conditions that are offered, and never demands a choice of weapons, never seeks strategic advantage from the lay of the land. But this time, it must be acknowledged, this precipitous about-face, this return from Egypt (or very nearly) like Napoleon, which no victorious Battle of the Nile can justify, has not seemed very fortunate; we have detected in it, or thought we did, let's say, a faint whiff of mystification. Some people have even gone so far as to utter, not without some semblance of justification, the word "gamble." Has Mr. Flaubert at least won this gamble? That is what we are about to examine in all candor, but without ever forgetting that the author is the son of a much to be lamented man whom we have all known, a professor at the École de Médecine in Rouen, who left his mark and his influence on his profession and in his province; or that this likeable son—whatever opinion you may proffer about what our over-hasty young are not afraid, boosted by friendship, to hail already as his "talent"—deserves, in any case, every consideration for the renowned simplicity of his narrations, always sure and perfectly executed—he, the very opposite of simplicity as soon as he picks up a pen!—by the refinement and invariable delicacy of his procedure.

The narrative begins with a scene that, if it had been better directed, could have given us a rather favorable idea of Mr. Flaubert, in that immediate and unexpected genre of the sketch, the study drawn from reality. We are at the Palais de Justice, in the Criminal Court, where the Lemoine case is underway, during an adjournment of the hearing. The windows have just been closed by order of the magistrate. And here an eminent lawyer assures me that the magistrate would in fact not be sitting there, but would more naturally and properly have withdrawn to the council chamber during the adjournment. This of course is only a minor detail. But how do you, who have just told us (as if you had actually counted them!) the number of elephants and onagers in the Carthaginian army, how do you hope, I ask you, to have your word believed when, for a reality that is so nearby, so easily verifiable, so basic even and not in the least detailed, you commit such blunders! But we'll move on: the author wanted an opportunity to describe the magistrate, and he didn't let one escape him. This magistrate has "a clown's face" (which is enough to make the reader lose interest), "a gown too narrow for his girth" (a rather clumsy characterization that portrays nothing), "aspirations to wit." We'll again overlook the clown's face! The author is of a school that never sees anything noble or decent in humanity. Mr. Flaubert, however, a thorough Norman if ever there was one, comes from a land of subtle chicanery and lofty cunning that has given France quite a few prominent lawyers and magistrates, I don't want to single out anyone here. Without even limiting ourselves to the boundaries of Normandy, the image of a magistrate such as Jeannin about whom Mr. Villemain has given us more than one delicate description, of a Mathieu Marais, a Saumaise, a Bouhier, even of the pleasant Patru, of one of these men who are distinguished by the wisdom of their advice and who are of such compelling merit, would be as interesting, I believe, and as true as that of the magistrate with "a clown's face" who is shown to us here. Enough about the clown's face! But if he has "aspirations to wit," how do you know about it, since he hasn't even opened his mouth yet? Similarly, a little later on, the author will point out to us, among the crowd he describes, a "reactionary." That is a common enough designation today. But here, I ask Mr. Flaubert again: "A reactionary? How can you recognize one at a distance? Who told you? How do you know about it?" The author evidently is amusing himself, and all these characteristics are invented on a whim. But that's nothing yet; we'll go on. The author continues portraying the public, or rather purely chosen "models" he has grouped together in his studio at his leisure: "Taking an orange out of his pocket, a black man . . ." Traveler! You use only words of truth, of "objectivity," you make a profession of it, you make a display of it; but, beneath this self-styled impersonality, how quickly we can recognize you, even if it's only from this black man, this orange, that parrot just now, who have just disembarked with you, all these accessories you have *brought back* with you that you hurry to *slap* onto your sketch—the most variegated, I declare, and the least authentic, the least lifelike one your brush has ever struggled with.

So the black man takes an orange out of his pocket, and by doing so, he "wins esteem"! Mr. Flaubert, I understand, means that in a crowd someone who can put himself to use and who shows off some advantage, even an ordinary one familiar to everyone—someone who takes out a goblet, for example, when someone else is drinking out of a bottle next to him; or a newspaper, if he is the only one who thought to buy one—that this person is immediately singled out, noticed and pointed out by others. But confess that when it comes down to it you don't mind, by risking this unusual and out of place expression of "winning esteem," insinuating that all esteem, even the highest and most sought-after, is not much more than that, that it is made of envy inspired by possessions that are at bottom without any intrinsic value. Well, we say to Mr. Flaubert, that is not true; esteem—and we know that the example will touch you, since it is only in literature that you belong to the school of insensitivity, of *impassivity*—is acquired by a whole life devoted to science, to humanity. Literature, once upon a time, could procure it also, when it was only the gauge and so to speak the flower of the mind's urbanity, of that entirely human disposition that can indeed have its predilections and its goals, but that allows, alongside images of vice and ridicule, those of innocence and virtue. Without going back to the ancients (who were much more "naturalist" than you will ever be, but who, on the painting we see in its material frame, always make a fully divine ray of light appear clearly, as if it were in the open air, which shines its light on the pediment and illumines the contrast), without going back to them, whether they go by the name of Homer or Moschus, Bion or Leonidas of Tarentum, not to mention more deliberate portrayals, tell us if you please, is this something different from what these same writers have always done, writers you do not fear to claim as your own? Saint-Simon above all, next to the atrocious and slanderous portraits of a Noailles or a Harlay, what great brushstrokes doesn't he use to show us, in its light and its proportion, the virtue of a Montal, a Beauvilliers, a Rancé, a Chevreuse? And even in that "Human Comedy," or the one so called, where Mr. de Balzac, with an almost mocking conceit, claims to outline "scenes" (actually entirely fabulous) "of Parisian and provincial life" (he, a man incapable of observation if ever there was one), compared with and almost making up for the Hulots, the Philippe Bridaus, the Balthazar Claes, as he calls them, and of whom your Narr'Havas and your Shahabarims have no reason to be envious, I admit, hasn't he imagined an Adeline Hulot, a Blanche de Mortsauf, a Marguerite de Solis?

Indeed, it would have astonished, and rightly so, the Jacquemonts, the Darus, the Mérimées, the Ampères, all those men of delicacy and scholarship who knew him so well and who did not think there was any need, for such a trifle, to make so many bells ring out, if someone had told them that the witty Stendhal, to whom we owe so many clear and fruitful views, so many apposite remarks, would pass as a novelist in our day. But finally, he is even *truer* than you are! And there is more reality in the smallest study by—I'll say Sénac or Meilhan, by Ramond or Althon Shée—than in yours, so laboriously inexact!—Don't you yourself feel how wrong it is?

Finally the hearing is resumed (all that is quite stripped of detail and argumentation), Werner's lawyer takes the stand, and Mr. Flaubert tells us that when he turns toward the magistrate he makes, each time, "such a profound bow that he was like a deacon leaving the altar." That there were such lawyers, even at the Paris bar, "kneeling," as the author says, before the court and the public prosecutor, is quite possible. But there are other kinds also—this, Mr. Flaubert does not want to know—and it wasn't so long ago that we heard the estimable Chaix d'Est-Ange (whose published speeches have lost not indeed any of their impetus and wit, but only their forensic pertinence) proudly respond to a haughty summing-up by the public prosecutor: "Here, at the bar, the counsel for the prosecution and I are equal—except in talent!" That day, the amiable jurist who could not indeed find around him the atmosphere, the divine resonance of the last age of the Republic, could still, just like Cicero, shoot the golden arrow.

But action, held back for a while, is spurred and hastened on. The defendant is introduced, and at first, upon seeing him, some people seem to yearn (always more guesswork!) for the wealth that would have allowed them to leave for distant lands with a once beloved woman, and escape to those hours the poet speaks of, that alone are worthy of being lived and in which one becomes inflamed sometimes for one's whole life, *vita dignior oetas*! This piece, read out loud—although it lacks some of that feeling of sweet and authentic impressions, in which a Monselet, a Frédéric Soulié have indulged with much charm—seems adequately harmonious and vague: "They would have known the cry of petrels, the coming of the fog, the rocking of ships, the formation of clouds." But, I ask you, what are petrels doing here? The author is again visibly starting to amuse himself— nay, we'll use the word—to mystify us. We don't need a degree in ornithology to know that the petrel is a very common bird on our shores, and that there is no need to invent the diamond and make a fortune just to meet one. A hunter who has often pursued it assures me that its cry has absolutely nothing special about it that could so strongly move someone hearing it. It is clear that the author had in mind only the felicity of the sentence. He decided the cry of the petrel would do the trick and so he quickly served it up to us. Mr. de Chateaubriand is the first person to have thus coaxed details added after the fact, and about whose truth he didn't trouble much, to appear in a studied framework. But he, even in his slightest annotation, had the divine gift, the word that made the image appear life-sized, forever, in his insight and his description; he possessed, as Joubert said, the talisman of the Enchanter. O ye descendents of Atala, descendents of Atala, we find you everywhere today, even on anatomists' dissection tables! Etc.

IV   BY HENRI DE RÉGNIER

I do not like the diamond at all. I see no beauty in it. The little beauty it adds to that of human faces is less an effect of its own than a reflection of theirs. It has neither the ocean clarity of the emerald, nor the unbounded azure of the sapphire. I prefer the smoky glint of the topaz to it, and above all the twilight charm of opals. They are emblematic and twofold. If moonlight makes half of their face iridescent, the other seems tinged by the pink and green glints of sunset. We are not so much amused by the colors it presents to us, as we are touched by the dreams it conjures up. To one who can encounter nothing beyond himself except the form of his own fate, they show an alternative and taciturn face.

There were many of them in the city where Hermas took me. The house we lived in was valuable more from the beauty of the site than from the comfort of the beings in it. The perspective of horizons was more carefully managed there than the furnishing of the premises was planned. It was more pleasant to daydream there than it was to sleep. It was more picturesque than comfortable. Overwhelmed by the heat during the day, the peacocks made their fateful, mocking cries heard all night long—cries that are, to tell the truth, more suitable for daydreaming than favorable to sleep. The sound of the bells kept one from finding sleep during the morning, failing the sleep that one can only really enjoy before daylight—though the later sleep at least makes up to a certain extent for the fatigue from having been completely deprived of the earlier. The majesty of the ceremonies whose hours their chimes announced was a poor recompense for the annoyance of being awakened at an hour when one is supposed to be asleep, if one wishes to be able, later on, to profit from the ensuing hours. The sole recourse then was to quit the cloth of the sheets and the feather of the pillow and go walk through the house. This undertaking, to tell the truth, although it had some charm, also presented danger. It was amusing without ceasing to be perilous. One would rather give up the pleasure of it than pursue the adventure. The parquet tiles that M. de Séryeuse had brought back from the islands were many-colored and disjointed, slippery and geometric. Their mosaic was brilliant and erratic. The pattern of its lozenges, now red, now black, offered to the gaze a more pleasing spectacle than the wooden floor—raised here, broken there—promised the step a sure gait.

The appeal of the walk one could have in the courtyard was not won by so many risks. One would go down into it around noon. The sun warmed the pavement, or the rain dripped from the rooftops. Sometimes wind made the weathervane creak. In front of the closed gate, monumental and covered with verdigris, a sculpted Hermes gave the shadow he projected the form of his caduceus. Dead leaves from nearby trees fell, swirling up to his heels, and folded onto the marble wings their wings of gold. Votive and potbellied, doves came to perch in the alcoves of the archivolt or on the splay of the pedestal, and often let fall a drab ball, flaky and gray. It splattered its intermittent, grainy mass on the gravel or on the grass, and, sticky with the grass it once had been, covered the grass abounding on the lawn and filling the footpath of what M. de Séryeuse called his garden.

Lemoine came often to stroll about there.

That is where I saw him for the first time. He seemed to be more aptly fitted in a lackey's smock than clad in a doctor's cap. The rogue claimed to be a doctor, though, in several sciences wherein it is more profitable to succeed than to which it is often prudent to devote oneself.

It was noon when his coach arrived, describing a circle in front of the steps. The pavement resounded with the team's hooves; a valet ran up to pull down the folding step. In the street, women crossed themselves. The north wind blew. At the foot of the marble Hermes, the caducean shadow had taken on an elusive and shifty aspect. Pursued by the wind, it seemed to be laughing. Bells rang out. Between the bronze volleys of a great bell, a peal of smaller bells, out of time with each other, hazarded their crystal choreography. In the garden, a swing creaked. Dry seeds lay on top of the sundial. The sun shone and disappeared by turns. Agatized by its light, the Hermes of the threshold became darker from the sun's obscuring than he would have been from its absence. Successive and ambiguous, the marmoreal face lived. A smile seemed to lengthen expiatory lips into the shape of a caduceus. The smell of willow, of pumice, of cineraria and marquetry escaped from the closed shutters of the office and from the half-open door of the vestibule. It made the dullness of the hour heavier. M. de Séryeuse and Lemoine continued to chat on the steps. One could hear an equivocal, shrill sound like a burst of furtive laughter. This was the gentleman's sword, which clinked against the glass alchemical retort. The feathered hat of the one safeguarded him better from the wind than the silken nightcap of the other. Lemoine had a cold. From his nose, which he forgot to wipe, a little mucus had fallen onto his shirtfront and onto his suit. Its viscous, warm core had slipped down the linen of one, but had adhered to the cloth of the other, and held the silvery, fluent fringe that dripped from it in suspense above the void. The sun, piercing them, confused the sticky mucus with the diluted solution. One could make out just the one single succulent, quivering mass, transparent and hardening; and in the ephemeral brilliance with which it decorated Lemoine's attire, it seemed to have fixed the prestige of a momentary diamond there, still hot, so to speak, from the oven from which it had emerged, and for which this unstable jelly, corrosive and alive as it was for one more instant, seemed at once, by its deceitful, fascinating beauty, to present both a mockery and a symbol.

V   IN "THE GONCOURT JOURNALS"

21 December 1907.

Dined with Lucien Daudet, who spoke with a touch
of mocking gusto about the fabulous diamonds seen
on the shoulders of Mme X . . . , diamonds being
pronounced by Lucien in extremely fine language, upon
my word, with an ever-artistic notation, with the savory
spelling out of his epithets marking the wholly superior
writer, as being despite everything a bourgeois stone,
a little silly, not at all comparable, for instance, to the
emerald or the ruby. And over dessert, Lucien let drop that
Lefebvre de Béhaine had told him, Lucien, that evening,
contrary to the opinion of the charming woman Mme de
Nadaillac, that a certain Lemoine has discovered the secret

of making diamonds. This would create, in the business world, according to Lucien, a furious commotion faced with the possible depreciation of still unsold diamond stocks, a commotion that could well end up reaching the judicial authorities, and bring about the imprisonment of this Lemoine for the rest of his days in some sort of *in pace*, for the crime of lèse-jewelry. This is more urgent than the story of Galileo, more modern, more open to the artistic evocation of a milieu, and all of a sudden I can see a fine subject for a play for us, a play that could contain strong things about the power of today's big business, a power that at bottom drives government and the law, opposing whatever calamitous thing any new invention has in store for it. Like a bouquet, they brought Lucien the news, presenting me with the denouement of the already sketched play, that their friend Marcel Proust had killed himself after the fall in diamond shares, a collapse that annihilated a part of his fortune. A curious person, Lucien assured us, that Marcel Proust, a being who lives entirely in the enthusiasm, in the *pious adoration*, of certain landscapes, certain books, a person for example who is completely enamored of the novels of Léon Daudet. And after a long silence, in the glow of after-dinner expansiveness, Lucien stated: "No, it's not because it concerns my brother, do not believe it, Monsieur de Goncourt, absolutely not. But finally the truth must be told." And he cited this characteristic that emerged prettily from the illuminated elaboration of his speech: "One day, a gentleman performed an immense favor for Marcel Proust, who, to thank him, brought him to the country to dine. But while they were chatting, the gentleman, who was none other than Zola, absolutely refused to acknowledge that there had been in France only one single truly great writer to whom only Saint-Simon came close, and that this writer was Léon Daudet. Upon which, my word! Proust, forgetting the gratitude he owed Zola, sent him flying ten steps backwards with a pair of blows, and knocked him flat on his back. The next day they fought, but, despite the intervention of Ganderax, Proust was firmly opposed to any reconciliation." And all of a sudden, in the clutter of the coffee cups being passed round, Lucien whispered in my ear, with a comic whine, this revelation: "Don't you see, Monsieur de Goncourt, if even despite *La Fourmilière* I'm not aware of this fashion, it's because I can *see* even the words people say, as if I were painting, in the *capture* of a nuance, with the same *sfumato* as Chanteloup's Pagoda." I left Lucien, my head all excited by this affair of the diamond and of suicide, as if spoonfuls of brain had just been poured into me. And on the staircase I met the new ambassador from Japan who, seeming ever so slightly freakish and *decadent*, making him resemble a samurai holding, above my folding Coromandel screen, the two pincers of a crayfish, graciously told me he had long been on assignment in the Honolulu Islands where reading our books, my brother's and mine, was the only thing capable of tearing the natives away from the pleasures of caviar, a reading that was prolonged till very late at night, in one go, with interludes consisting only of chewing some cigars of the country that come encased in long glass tubes, which are supposed to protect them during the crossing from a certain distemper the sea gives them. And the minister confessed to me his taste for our books, admitting he had known in Hong Kong a very great lady there who had only two books on her night table: *La Fille Elisa* and *Robinson Crusoe*.

22 December.

I awoke from my four o'clock siesta with the presentiment of some piece of bad news. I had dreamt that the tooth that had made me suffer so when Cruet pulled it out, five years ago, had grown in again. And straightway Pélagie came in, with this news brought by Lucien Daudet, news she hadn't come to tell me earlier so as not to disturb my nightmare: Marcel Proust has not killed himself, Lemoine has invented nothing at all, is nothing but a conjurer who isn't even very clever, a kind of Robert-Houdin with no hands. Just our luck! For once the present workaday, dull life had *taken on some artistry*, offered us a subject for a play! Facing Rodenbach, who was waiting for me to wake up, I was not able to contain my disappointment, though I recovered myself sufficiently to become animated, to give vent to some already-composed tirades that the false news of the discovery and of the suicide had inspired in me, false news that was more artistic, *truer*, than the too-optimistic and *public* outcome, an outcome à la Sarcey, which Lucien told Pélagie was the real one. As for me, it was nothing but protest that I whispered for an hour to Rodenbach about the bad luck that has always pursued us, my brother and me, making the biggest events into the smallest, a people's revolution into the sniffles of a stage prompter, so many obstacles raised against the forward progress of our works. Now this time the jeweler's guild has to get mixed up in it! Then Rodenbach confessed to me the nub of his thinking, which is that December has always been unlucky for us, for my brother and me, a month that saw our pastimes brought to court, and the failure of *Henriette Maréchal* planned by the press, and the cold sore I had on my tongue the day before the only speech I ever had to give, a cold sore that made people say I hadn't dared to speak at the tomb of Vallès, when I was the one who had asked to do so—a whole company of mischances that, this man from the artistic North that is Rodenbach said superstitiously, should make us avoid undertaking anything at all this month. Then, when I interrupted the cabbalistic theories of the author of *Bruges la Morte* so as to go put on the tailcoat required for dinner at the Princess', I said to him, leaving him at the door of my dressing room: "So then, Rodenbach, you advise me to reserve this month for my death!"

VI "THE LEMOINE AFFAIR"
BY MICHELET

The diamond can be mined at strange depths (1300 meters). To bring the most brilliant stone back, which alone can support the fire of a woman's gaze (in Afghanistan, a diamond is called "the eye of flame"), you will have to descend endlessly into the dark kingdom. How many times will Orpheus wander astray before he brings Eurydice back to daylight! But be not discouraged! If your heart loses its resolve, the stone is there, and with its very distinct flame seems to say, "Courage, one more blow with your pickaxe, and I am yours." But one moment of hesitation, and you are dead. There is salvation only in speed. A touching dilemma. To resolve it, many lives wore themselves out in the Middle Ages. It was posited more harshly at the beginning of the twentieth century (December 1907—January 1908). Someday I will relate that magnificent Lemoine affair, the greatness of which no contemporary has suspected; I will show the little man, with clumsy hands, his eyes burning with the terrible search, a Jew probably (M. Drumont said so not without plausibility; even today the Lemoustiers—a contraction of Monastère—are not uncommon in the Dauphiné, the chosen land of Israel throughout the whole Middle Ages), leading all of Europe's politics for three months, forcing proud England to consent to a trade treaty that was ruinous for it, to save its threatened mines, its discredited companies. No doubt it would pay his weight in gold for us to yield the man up. His release on bail, the greatest conquest of modern times (Sayous, Batbie), was three times refused. The deductive German in front of his stein of beer, seeing the shares in De Beers go down day by day, took heart again (the Harden retrial, Polish law, refusal to answer the Reichstag). Touching immolation of the Jew throughout the ages! "You slander me, stubbornly accuse me of treason against all evidence, on land, on sea (Dreyfus affair, Ullmo affair); well then! I give you my gold (see the great development of Jewish banks at the end of the nineteenth century), and more than gold, what you could still not buy with the weight of gold: the diamond." —Grave lesson; very sadly did I meditate on it during that winter of 1908 when nature itself, abdicating all violence, became treacherous instead. Never were there fewer harsh cold spells, but there was a fog that even at noon the sun could not contrive to pierce. What's more, the temperature was very mild—all the more lethal. Many deaths—more than in the preceding ten years—and, in January, violets under the snow. One's mind was quite disturbed by this Lemoine affair, which quite correctly appeared to me immediately as an episode in the great struggle of wealth against science; every day I went to the Louvre where instinctively the people linger, more often than they do before da Vinci's Mona Lisa, at the Crown diamonds. More than once I've had trouble getting close to them. It goes without saying, this study attracted me, but I did not like it. And my reason? I did not sense any life in it. Always that has been my strength, my weakness too, this need for life. At the high point of the reign of Louis XIV, when absolutism seems to have killed all freedom in France, for two long years—more than a century—(1680-1789), peculiar headaches every day made me think that I was going to be forced to abandon my history. I didn't really recover my strength until the Tennis Court Oath (20 June 1789). I felt similarly disturbed before this strange realm of crystallization that is the world of the stone. Here there is no more of the flexibility of the flower that, at the most arduous of my botanical researches, very timidly—all the better—never stopped giving me courage: "Have confidence, fear nothing, you are still in the midst of life, in history."

IN THE WEEKLY THEATER REVIEW
BY M. ÉMILE FAGUET

The author of *Le Détour* and *Le Marché*—namely M.
Henri Bernstein—has just had a play, or rather an
ambiguous combination of tragedy and vaudeville,
performed by the actors of the Gymnase, which may
not be his *Athalie* or his *Andromaque* [Racine], his
L'Amour Veille [Henry Roussel] or his *Les Sentiers de la
Vertu* [Robert de Flers], but yet is something like his
Nicomède [Corneille], which is not at all, as you may have
heard, a completely contemptible play and is not at all
entirely a disgrace to the human spirit. Although the
play has reached, I will not say beyond the heavens, but

at least up to the highest clouds, where there is some exaggeration, it has done so with legitimate success, since M. Bernstein's play abounds with improbabilities, but on a background of truth. That is where *The Lemoine Affair* differs from *La Rafale*, and, in general, from all of M. Bernstein's tragedies, as well as from a good half of Euripides' comedies, which abound in truths, but on a background of improbability. What's more, this is the first time a play by M. Bernstein involves actual people, from whom he had held back till now. The swindler Lemoine, then, wanting to dupe people with his alleged discovery of how to make diamonds, goes to see . . . the greatest diamond-mine owner in the world. As implausibility goes, you will agree that that is a rather considerable one. This is one thing. At the very least, you expect that that magnate, who has all the greatest affairs in the world to occupy him, will send Lemoine packing, just as the prophet Nehemiah said from atop the ramparts of Jerusalem to those who held out a ladder for him to come down, *Non possum descendere, magnum opus facio.* That would have been the perfect response. But not at all, he hurries to use the ladder. The only difference is that instead of going down, he climbs up it. A bit youthful, this Werner. This is not a role for M. Coquelin the younger, but rather for M. Brulé. And now for another thing. Note that Lemoine does not make a gift of this secret, which naturally is nothing but a trifling quack recipe. He sells it to him for two million francs, and still makes him think it's a steal:

> *Admire my kindnesses and the little sold to you*
> *The wonderful treasure my hand dispenses to you.*
>> *O great power*
>> *Of the Panacea!*
>>> (see Molière, *L'Amour Médecin*.)

Which doesn't change much, all in all, of the implausibility of No. 1, but doesn't make the implausibility of No. 2 much worse. But finally, anything goes! My God, note that until now we have been following the author who is a pretty good dramatist. We are told that Lemoine discovered the secret of diamond-making. We know nothing of that, after all; we are just told it, we want to go along with it, we're game. Werner, the great diamond expert, was taken in, and Werner, the crafty financier, paid up. And we are taken in right along with him. A great English scholar, half-physicist, half-nobleman, an English lord, as they say (but no, Madame, all lords are English, so an English lord is a pleonasm; don't start that again, no one heard you), swears that Lemoine has genuinely discovered the philosopher's stone. We can't go any further than we've gone. Boom! Suddenly the jewelers recognize Lemoine's diamonds as the very stones they sold him, and that they come *precisely from Werner's own mine*. A bit much, that. The diamonds *still have the marks the jewelers had put on them*. Worse and worse:

> In the marked diamond that comes thus out of the
>> oven,
> I no longer recognize the author of *Le Détour*.

Lemoine is arrested, Werner demands his money back, the English lord doesn't say one word more; all of a sudden we've stopped going along with it, and as always, in such cases, we are furious at having gone on for so long, so we shift our anger to . . . Egad! The author is there for something, I think. Werner immediately asks the judge to demand the requisition of the envelope where the famous secret is enclosed. The judge assents right away. No one more amiable than this judge. But Lemoine's lawyer tells the judge that such an action is illegal. The judge immediately desists; no one more pliable than this judge. As for Lemoine, he absolutely wants to wander along with the judge, the lawyers, the experts, etc., over to Amiens where his factory is, to prove to them that he can make diamonds. And every time the amiable, pliable judge repeats to him that he swindled Werner, Lemoine replies, "Let's stop talking and go for a stroll." To which the judge gives him the reply, "The stroll, in my opinion, is a dreary thing." No one better versed in Molière's plays than this judge. Etc.

If Lemoine had actually made a diamond, he would no doubt have satisfied, to a certain extent, that coarse materialism with which whoever intends to meddle in human affairs must reckon; he certainly would not have given to souls in love with the ideal that element of exquisite spirituality by which, after so long a time, we are still sustained. That in any case is what the magistrate who was appointed to question him seems, with a rare keenness, to have understood. Every time that Lemoine, with the smile we can imagine, proposed that he come to Lille, to his factory, where they could see if he did or did not know how to make a diamond, the judge Le Poittevin, with exquisite tact, did not let him continue, indicating to him with a word, sometimes with a rather pointed joke,[1] but still restrained by a rare feeling for moderation, that this was not what was at question, that the issue lay elsewhere. Nothing, in any case, authorizes us to assert that even at that moment when, feeling his case was lost (as early as January, with no longer any doubt remaining about the sentence, the accused naturally clung to the most fragile last hope), Lemoine ever claimed that he knew how to make diamonds. The place he offered to lead the experts, which translations call a "factory," a word that could have lent itself to misinterpretations, was located at the far end of the valley which extends for more than thirty kilometers and terminates in Lille. Even these days, after all the deforestation it has undergone, it is a veritable garden, planted with poplars and willow trees, strewn with fountains and flowers. At the height of summer, the coolness there is delicious. It is hard for us to imagine today how it has lost its groves of chestnut trees, its copses of hazel trees and vines, all the fertility that made it an enchanting place to visit during Lemoine's time. An Englishman who lived at that time, John Ruskin, whom unfortunately we read now only in the pitifully insipid translation that Marcel Proust has bequeathed to us, extols the grace of its poplars, the icy coolness of its springs. The traveler, having just emerged from the solitudes of the Beauce and the Sologne, which are always made desolate by an implacable sun, could truly believe, when he saw their transparent water

---

1 *Trial*, Volume II *passim*, see especially "country," etc.

sparkling through the foliage, that some genie, touching the ground with his magic wand, made the diamond too gush forth from it. Lemoine, probably, never meant to say anything else. It seems he wanted, not without anxiety, to make use of all the delays the French law possesses, and which easily allowed the investigation to be prolonged until mid-April, when that part of the country is especially delicious. In the hedges, the lilac and the wild rose, the white and pink hawthorn, are all in bloom, and cover every path with embroidery of an incomparable freshness of tones, where the various sorts of birds of that countryside come to mingle their songs. The golden oriole, the titmouse, the blue-headed nightingale, sometimes the waxbill, answer each other from branch to branch. The hills, clad in the distance with the pink flowers of fruit trees, unfurl their ravishingly delicate curves against the blue sky. By the shores of rivers that are still the great charm of that region, but where sawmills today keep up an unbearable noise at all hours, the silence would have been disturbed only by the sudden rise of one of those little trout whose rather bland flesh is still the most exquisite of delights for the Picardy peasant. No doubt that by leaving the furnace of the Palais de Justice, experts and judges would have experienced just like everyone else the eternal mirage of that beautiful water that the noonday sun truly sets with diamonds. To lie down by the river's edge, to greet with one's laughter a small boat whose wake ruffles the changing silk of the water, to extract a few azure scraps from that sapphire gorget that is the peacock's neck, gaily to chase young washerwomen to their scrubbing-stones while singing a popular tune,[2] to soak in soap suds a reed pipe carved from stubble into the shape of Pan's flute, to watch bubbles bead up there that combine to form the delicious colors of Iris' scarf and to call that "threading pearls," to join choruses sometimes holding each other by the hand, to listen to the nightingale sing, to watch the shepherd's star rise—those were undoubtedly the pleasures to which Lemoine counted on inviting the honorable gentlemen Le Poittevin, Bordas and company, pleasures of a truly idealistic race, where everything ends in song, where since the end of the nineteenth century the slight drunkenness of the wine of Champagne seems even too coarse, where one seeks gaiety only from the vapor that, from sometimes incalculable depths, rises to the surface of a faintly mineral spring.

The name "Lemoine"—"Monk"—should not, however, give us the notion of one of those severe ecclesiastical attitudes that would have made Lemoine himself not at all susceptible to such poetically

---

2 Some of those deliciously naïve songs have been preserved for us. It is generally a scene borrowed from daily life that the singer gaily recounts. The words of "Zizi Panpan," by themselves, which are almost always cut off at regular intervals, bring nothing but a rather vague sense to the mind. It was probably pure rhythmic indications supposed to mark the measure for an ear that would otherwise have been tempted to forget it, perhaps even simply an admiring exclamation, uttered upon seeing Juno's bird, as these often-repeated words *les plumes de paon* (the peacock's feathers) would tend to have us think, which follow them without much pause.

enchanting impressions. It was probably only a nickname, the kind many people have, perhaps a simple pet name that the reserved manners of the young scholar, with his life scarcely given over to worldly dissipations, had quite naturally brought to the lips of frivolous people. Besides, it seems to me that we should not attach much importance to these epithets, many of which seem to have been chosen by chance, probably to distinguish two people who might otherwise have been confused with each other. The slightest nuance, or some distinction that's often completely irrelevant, suffices to identify the man. The simple epithet of *senior*, or *junior*, added to the same name, seemed sufficient. It is often a question in documents of that era of a certain *Coquelin the Elder* who seems to have been a kind of proconsular individual, perhaps a wealthy administrator like Crassus or Murena. Without any definite text allowing us to affirm that he served in person, he held a distinguished position in the order of the Legion of Honor, created expressly by Napoleon to reward military merit. This nickname of "the Elder" may have been given him to distinguish him from another Coquelin, an esteemed actor, called *Coquelin the Younger*, without our being able to discover whether there was in fact an actual difference in age between them. It seems they simply wanted to use that method to honor the distance that still existed at that time between the actor and the politician, the man who had performed civic responsibilities. Perhaps they quite simply wanted to avoid any confusion on the electoral lists.

. . . A society where beautiful women, where noblemen of high birth, adorn their bodies with real diamonds is condemned to irremediable coarseness. The worldly man, the man for whom the dry rationality, the entirely superficial brilliance provided by classical education, are enough, might take pleasure in it. Truly pure souls, minds passionately attached to the good and the true, would experience an unbearable sensation of suffocation in such a society. Such customs could exist in the past. We will not see them again. During Lemoine's time, according to all appearances, they had long ago become obsolete. The dull collection of implausible stories which bears the title *The Human Comedy* by Balzac is perhaps the work neither of one single man nor of one single era. Yet his still unshaped style, his ideas all marked by an old-fashioned absolutism, allow us to place its publication at least two centuries before Voltaire. However, Mme de Beauséant, who, in these insipidly dry fictions, personifies the perfectly distinguished woman, already shows scorn for the wives of nouveau riche businessmen appearing in public adorned with precious stones. It is probable that in Lemoine's day a woman anxious to please was content to add some leaves to her hair where some dewdrop still trembled, as sparkling as the rarest diamond. In the cento of disparate poems entitled *Songs of the Streets and the Woods*, which is commonly attributed to Victor Hugo, although it is probably a little later than that, the words "diamonds" and "pearls" are used indiscriminately to portray the glittering of drops of water gushing from a murmuring spring, sometimes from a simple shower. In a kind of erotic little romance that recalls the *Song of Songs*, the bride says in so many words to the Husband that she wants no other diamonds than the drops of dew. Probably it is a question here of a generally accepted custom, not of an individual preference. This last hypothesis is, moreover, excluded in advance by the perfect banality of these little pieces that have been ascribed to the name of Hugo by virtue no doubt of the same desire for publicity that must have made Qoheleth (*Ecclesiastes*) decide to adorn his spiritual maxims with the respected name of Solomon, who was much in vogue at that time.

Moreover, if they find out tomorrow how to make a diamond, I will undoubtedly be one of the least likely people to attach much importance to it. That has a lot to do with my education. I had scarcely reached the age of forty, when at the public meetings of the Society of Jewish Studies, I met some of the people liable to be strongly impressed by news of such a discovery. At Tréguier, with my first masters, then later on at Issy, at Saint-Sulpice, this news would have been met with the most extreme indifference, perhaps with an ill-concealed scorn. Whether or not Lemoine found a way to make diamonds, we cannot imagine how little that would have affected my sister Henriette, my uncle Pierre, M. Le Hir, or M. Carbon. At bottom, I have always remained on this point, as well as on many others, an old-fashioned disciple of Saint Tudual and Saint Colomban. This has often led me to utter, in all things having to do with luxury, unforgivably naïve remarks. At my age, I would not even be capable of going to buy a ring at a jeweler's. Ah! It's not in our Trégorrois that young ladies receive from their fiancés, like the Shulamite, strings of pearls, expensive necklaces set with silver, "*vermiculata argento*." For me, the only precious stones that would still be capable of making me leave the Collège de France, despite my rheumatism, and take to the sea, but only if one of my old Breton saints consented to take me out on his apostolic bark, are the ones the fishermen in Saint-Michel-en-Grève sometimes glimpse at the bottom of the sea during fair weather, where the city of Ys used to stand, set in the stained-glass windows of its hundred drowned cathedrals.

. . . No doubt cities like Paris, London, Paris-Plage, Bucharest, will look less and less like the city that appeared to the presumed author of the Fourth Gospel, the city built of emerald, jacinth, beryl, chrysoprase, and other precious stones, with twelve doors each formed from a single fine pearl. But living in such a city would soon make us yawn with boredom, and who knows if the incessant contemplation of a setting like the one in which John's *Apocalypse* unfolds might risk making the universe perish suddenly from a brainstorm? More and more the *fundabo te in saphiris et ponam jaspidem propugnacula tua et omnes terminus tuos in lapides desiderabiles* will appear to us as a simple figure of speech, like a promise kept for the last time at St. Mark's in Venice. It is clear that if he supposed he ought not deviate from the principles of urban architecture according to Revelation, and if he meant to apply to the letter the *Fundamentum primum calcedonius . . . , duodecimum amethystus*, then my eminent friend M. Bouvard would risk postponing indefinitely the continuation of Boulevard Haussmann.

Patience, then! Humanity, patience. Rekindle tomorrow the furnace that has already gone out a thousand times whence the diamond might one day emerge! With a good humor that the Eternal can envy in you, perfect the crucible where you will make carbon rise to temperatures unknown to Lemoine and Bertholet. Tirelessly repeat the *sto ad ostium et pulso*, without knowing if a voice will ever reply: *Veni, veni, coronaberis*. Your story has now entered a path from which the stupid fantasies of the vain and the aberrant will never contrive to make you stray. The day Lemoine, by an exquisite play on words, called simple drops of water valuable only in their freshness and limpidity "precious stones," the cause of idealism was won forever. He did not make a diamond: he made the price of an ardent imagination, of perfect simplicity of heart, incontestable—things important in other ways for the future of the planet. They will lose their value only on the day that a deeper knowledge of cerebral localizations and the progress of brain surgery allow us easily to set in motion the infinitely delicate mechanisms that awaken modesty and an innate sense of beauty. On that day, the free thinker, the man who has a high idea of virtue, would see the value on which he placed all his hopes undergo an irresistible movement of depreciation. Surely the believer who hopes to exchange a virtue he bought cheaply with indulgences for a share of eternal felicities, is desperately attached to an untenable proposition. But it is clear the virtue of the free thinker would scarcely be worth anything at all the day it becomes merely the compulsory result of the success of an intracranial operation.

Men of a given era see among the various personalities who by turns seek out public attention all sorts of differences that they think are enormous, yet that posterity will not notice. We are all rough drafts where the genius of one epoch is prelude to a masterpiece that it will probably never execute. For us, between two personalities like the honorable M. Denys Cochin and Lemoine, the dissimilarities leap to the eye. They might perhaps escape the Seven Sleepers, if they awoke a second time from the sleep they fell into in the reign of the Emperor Decius which was thought to last a scant three hundred seventy-two years. The Messianic point of view can no longer be our own. Less and less does the privation of some gift or other of the mind seem to us to deserve the wonderful curses it inspired in the unknown author of the Book of Job. "Compensation"—this word, which dominates Emerson's philosophy, could well be the last word of all sound judgment, the judgment of the true agnostic. The Comtesse de Noailles, if she is the author of the poems attributed to her, left an extraordinary work, a hundred times superior to Qoheleth, or to Béranger's songs. But what a false position that must have given her in society! She seems, moreover, to have understood this perfectly and to have led in the country, perhaps not without some ennui,[3] an entirely simple, retired life, in the little orchard that usually serves as her interlocutor. The excellent singer Polin might perhaps be a little lacking in metaphysics; but he possesses a quality that is a thousand times more precious and which neither the son of Sirach nor Jeremiah ever knew: a delicious joviality, exempt from the slightest trace of affectation, etc.

---

3 We may wonder if this exile was indeed voluntary, and if we should not rather see in it one of those decisions of authority similar to the one that prevented Mme de Staël from returning to France, perhaps because of some law, the text of which has not reached us, and which forbade women from writing. The exclamations repeated a thousand times in these poems with such monotonous insistence: "Ah! To leave! Ah! To leave! To take the train that whistles as it rushes onward!" (*Occident.*) "Let me go, let me go." (*Tumulte dans l'aurore.*) "Ah! Let me leave." (*Les héros.*) "Ah! To return to my city, to see the Seine flow within its noble banks. To say to Paris: I'm on my way, I'll be back, I'm coming!" etc., show clearly that she was not free to take the train. Some verses where she seems to be adapting to her solitude: "What if already my sky is too divine for me," etc., have obviously been added afterwards to try to disarm the authorities' suspicions by a semblance of submission.

Wedding of Talleyrand-Périgord.—Successes won by the Imperials at Château-Thierry, exceedingly inferior.—Le Moine, by La Mouchi, is introduced to the Regent.—Conversation I had with M. the Duc d'Orléans on this subject. He is resolved to bring up the affair with the Duc de Guiche.—Fantasies of the Murats on the rank of foreign prince.—Conversation of the Duc de Guiche with M. the Duc d'Orléans on Le Moine, at the parvulo given at Saint-Cloud for the King of England traveling incognito in France.—Unprecedented presence of the Comte de Fels at this parvulo.—Journey to France of an Infante of Spain, very remarkable.

That year took place the wedding of good lady Blumenthal with L. de Talleyrand-Périgord, who has been mentioned many times in the course of these Memoirs, with emphatic and well-deserved praise. The Rohans hosted the wedding, which was attended by people of quality. He did not want his wife to remain seated during the wedding, but she presumed to use a slipcover on her chair and incontinently had herself addressed as Duchess of Montmorency, which did not advance her in the least. The campaign continued against the Imperials who despite the revolts in Hungary caused by the high price of bread won some successes at Château-Thierry. It was there that for the first time we saw the impropriety of M. de Vendôme, publicly called "Highness." The scourge reached even the Murats, and did not fail to cause me anxieties against which I kept up my spirits only with difficulty, so that I had gone far from the court, to spend the Easter fortnight at La Ferté in the company of a gentleman who had served in my regiment and was highly regarded by the late King, when on the eve of Low Sunday a letter that Mme de Saint-Simon sent advised me to go to Meudon as quickly as possible for an important affair concerning M. the Duc d'Orléans. At first I thought it was a matter of the affair of the false Marquis de Ruffec, which has been noted in its place; but Biron had skimmed it, and from a few words Mme de Saint-Simon dropped, about gems and some rogue named Le Moine, I was quite certain that it was not one more problem of those alembics that, without the influence I exercised with the chancellor, had been so close to getting—I scarcely dare write it—M. the Duc d'Orléans locked up in the Bastille. We do in fact know that this unfortunate prince, having no true or extensive knowledge about births, family histories, or what truth there might be in pretensions, the absurdity that bursts forth from some people and lets the bedrock be glimpsed which is nothing at all, the brilliance of marriages and offspring, even less the art of distinguishing in his courtesy between higher and lower rank, or of charming others with the obliging word that shows one knows what is the real and enduring, dare I say, *intrinsecum* of genealogies, this prince had never learned how to enjoy himself at court, had therefore seen himself abandoned by what he had first turned away from, to such an extent that he had fallen, although a first-rate prince of the blood, to immersing himself in chemistry, in painting, in the Opera, the musicians from which often came to bring him their scores and their violins which held no secrets for him. We also saw with what pernicious art his enemies, and above all the Maréchal de Villeroy, had used his taste for chemistry against him, so out of place, during the strange death of the Dauphin and the Dauphine. Far from the frightful rumors that had been spread at the time with pernicious cleverness by anyone who came close to the Maintenon causing M. the Duc d'Orléans to repent of researches that were so little suited to a man of his breeding, we saw that on the contrary he went on pursuing them with Mirepoix, every night, in the quarries of Montmartre, working on coal that he heated with a blowtorch, where, by a contradiction that can be conceived of only as Providence's chastisement of this prince, he drew an abominable glory from not believing in God and confessed to me more than once that he had hoped to see the devil.

The Mississippi business had come to an abrupt end and the Duc d'Orléans came, against my advice, to pronounce his useless edict against gemstones. Those who owned some, after having shown eagerness and experienced difficulty in selling them, preferred to keep them by hiding them, which is much easier to do with gems than with money, so that despite all the sleights of hand and various threats of imprisonment, the financial situation had been only very slightly and very temporarily bettered. Le Moine knew this and thought he could make M. the Duc d'Orléans believe the situation would improve if he could persuade him that it was possible to make diamonds. He hoped at the same time thereby to flatter that prince's detestable tastes for chemistry, and thus gain his favor. This did not happen right away. But it was not difficult to approach M. the Duc d'Orléans provided one possessed neither high birth, nor virtue. We have seen what the dinners of those ruffians were, from which only good company were kept at a distance by careful exclusion. Le Moine, however, who had spent his life buried in the most obscure debauchery and did not know even one person at court who could call him by name, did not know whom to address in order to win access to the Palais Royal; but in the end, La Mouchi did the honors. He saw M. the Duc d'Orléans, told him that he knew how to make diamonds, and this prince, naturally credulous, fell for it. I thought at first that the best thing was to approach the King through Maréchal. But I feared breaking the news, which might hurt the one I wanted to save, so I resolved to go straight to the Palais Royal. I ordered my carriage, simmering with impatience, and I threw myself into it like a man who is taking leave of his senses. I had often said to M. the Duc d'Orléans that I was not a man to importune him with my advice, but that when I had any, if I dared say, to give him, he should believe it was urgent, so I asked him to do me the good favor of receiving me right away since I had never been of a humor to wait quietly in the anteroom. His chief valets could have saved me that trouble, in any case, because of the knowledge I had of the whole inner workings of his court. But that day he had me come in as soon as my carriage had pulled up in the inmost courtyard of the Palais Royal, which was always full of those to whom entrance should have been forbidden, since, by a shameful prostitution of all dignities and by the deplorable weakness of the Regent, those who were of the lowest quality, who did not even fear making their way up in long coats, could penetrate the court just as easily as dukes and almost on the same standing. Those are matters one might treat as being of no consequence, but to which men of the previous reign would not have given credence, who, fortunately for them, had died promptly enough not to witness such things. Immediately ushered into the presence of the Regent whom I found without a single one of his surgeons or other domestics, and after I had greeted him with a very perfunctory bow that was returned me in exactly the same way: "Well, what is it now?" he asked awkwardly, as if humoring me. "Since you order me to speak, Monsieur," I said heatedly, keeping my gaze fixed on his own, which could not sustain it, "it is only that you are in the process of losing in the eyes of everyone the little esteem and consideration"—those were the very words I used—"that most of society has kept for you."

And, sensing him deeply wounded (because of which, despite what I knew of his insouciance, I conceived some hope), without pausing, so as to unburden myself once and for all of the unfortunate medicine I had to make him swallow, and so as not to give him time to interrupt me, I represented to him with the most frightful detail with what abandon he lived at the court, and how advanced this neglect —the right word had to be said, this contempt—had become in a few years; how these would be increased by the intrigues that would not fail to use the so-called inventions of Le Moine to cast wicked accusations against the Duc d'Orléans himself that might be absurd, but dangerous down to the last point; I reminded him—and I still tremble sometimes, at night when I wake up, when I think of the boldness I had in using these very words—that he had been accused many times of poisoning the princes who barred his way to the throne; that this great pile of gemstones they would have accepted as real would help him more easily attain the throne of Spain, for which reason no one doubted there was an entente between him, the Viennese court, the Emperor, and Rome; that because of the detestable authority of Rome he rejected Mme d'Orléans, and that it was a blessing from Providence for him that her recent confinements were fortunate, since otherwise the wicked rumors of poisoning would have been renewed; that to tell the truth, for desiring the death of Madame his wife, he was not like his brother guilty of Italian taste—these were my very terms—but that it was the only vice of which he was not accused (along with not having clean hands), since his relations with Mme la Duchesse de Berry seemed to many not to be those of a father; that if he had not inherited the abominable taste of Monsieur for all the rest, he was indeed his son from the habit of the perfumes that had put him out of favor with the king who could not bear them, and later on had favored the frightful rumors of having made an attempt on the Dauphine's life, and by having always put into practice the detestable maxim of dividing to conquer with the help of repeating rumors from one person to another which were the plague of his court, as they had been that of Monsieur, his father, where they had prevented a unified reign: that he had preserved for Monsieur's favorites a consideration that he did not grant to another, and that it was they—I did not force myself to name Effiat—who, aided by Mirepoix and La Mouchi, had cleared the way for Le Moine; that having as his only shield only men who no longer counted for anything after the death of Monsieur and who during his life had only amounted to anything because of the horrid conviction everyone had, even the king who had thus arranged to marry Mme d'Orléans, that one could obtain anything from them by means of money, and from him by those in whose clutches he was, no one feared attacking him by the most odious, the most intimate calumny, that it was high time, if indeed there still was time, for him finally to recover his grandeur and there was only one way to do that: to take measures in the greatest secrecy to have Le Moine arrested and, as soon as the thing was decided, not to delay the execution of it, and not to let him ever return to France.

M. the Duc d'Orléans, who had merely exclaimed once or twice at the beginning of this speech, had afterwards kept the silence of a man devastated by such a great blow; but my last words finally made a few of his own come out of his mouth. He was not spiteful, and resolution was not his strong point:

"What, then!" he said to me in a complaining tone, "Arrest him? But what if his invention happens to be real?"

"What's this, Monsieur," I replied, utterly surprised at such an extreme and pernicious blindness, "how can you think that, and so soon after having been disabused about the writing of the false Marquis de Ruffec? But really, if you have even one doubt, call for the man who knows more than anyone else in France about chemistry and all the sciences, as has been recognized by the academies and by astronomers; his character and birth, and the stainless life that has accompanied him, are your guarantee of his word." He understood that I was talking about the Duc de Guiche, and with the joy of a man entangled in conflicting choices, from whom another man has removed the anxiety of having to make the right one:

"Excellent! We both had the same idea," he said. "Guiche will decide, but I cannot see him today. You know that the King of England, traveling quite incognito under the name of the Earl of Stanhope, is coming tomorrow to talk with the King about matters in Holland and Germany; I'm giving him a party at Saint-Cloud, to which Guiche is invited. You will speak to him and me both, after dinner. But are you sure he'll come?" he added in an embarrassed way.

I understood that he didn't dare summon the Duc de Guiche to the Palais Royal, where, as you may imagine from the kind of people that M. the Duc d'Orléans saw, with whom Guiche was not at all acquainted, aside from Besons and me, he came as seldom as he could, knowing that it was the libertines who ranked first there rather than men like himself. Also the Regent, always fearing the duke would shower him with reproaches, lived in constant suspicion and reserve towards him. Very careful to give everyone his due and not being unaware of what was due the true son of Monsieur, Guiche visited him only on special occasions, and I do not think anyone had seen him at the Palais Royal since he had come to pay him his respects upon the death of Monsieur, and the pregnancy of Mme d'Orléans. Even then he stayed only a short while, with indeed an air of respect, but as one who knew how to show with discernment that he was addressing, not the person, but the rank of a first prince of the blood. M. the Duc d'Orléans sensed this and did not fail to be affected by so bitter and cutting a treatment.

As I was leaving the Palais Royal, deeply sorry to see a project consigned to the parvulo[4] at Saint-Cloud, something which might not even be carried out at all if it wasn't done at the very instant, so great were the habitual fickleness and sophistries of M. the Duc d'Orléans, a curious adventure befell me that I relate here only because it foretold only too well what would happen at the parvulo. I had just climbed into my carriage where Mme de Saint-Simon was awaiting me, when I was utterly surprised to see about to pass in front of it the carriage of S. Murat, so well-known by armies for his valor, and for that of his entire family. His sons had covered themselves with honor by traits worthy of antiquity; one, who lost a leg, shines everywhere with beauty; another son died, leaving parents who were inconsolable; so much so that although displaying pretensions as unbearable as those of the Bouillons, they did not lose the esteem of respectable people as the Bouillons had.

I might have been less surprised by this matter of the carriage perhaps, if I had remembered some rather strange suggestions, such as at one of the last *marlis*[5]

---

4   An exclusive dinner party given by Louis XIV at Meudon; the term was coined by Saint-Simon. — Trans.
5   Dinner parties given by Louis XIV at the Château de Marly. — Trans.

where Mme Murat had tried the ruse of making way
for Mme de Saint-Simon, but very equivocally and
without putting on a show of rank, saying that there was
less air there, that Mme de Saint-Simon feared air but
that Fagon on the other hand had prescribed it for her;
Mme de Saint-Simon had not let herself be taken in by
these bold words and had briskly replied that she chose
that place not because she feared the air, but because
it was her place and that if Mme Murat made as if to
have one, she and the other duchesses would go ask
Mme the Duchesse de Bourgogne to complain to the
King. To which Princess Murat had said not a word,
except that she knew what was due to Mme de Saint-
Simon, who was strongly applauded for her firmness by
the duchesses present and by the Princess d'Espinoy.
Despite this very singular *marli*, which had remained in
my memory and where I clearly grasped that Mme Murat
had wanted to test the waters, I believed this time in a
mistake, so strong did the pretension seem to me; but
seeing that Prince Murat's horses were getting ahead, I
sent a gentleman to ask him to make them fall back, to
whom it was replied that Prince Murat would have done
so with great pleasure had he been alone, but that he
was with Mme Murat, and some vague words about the
fancy of a foreign prince. Deeming that this was not the
place to demonstrate the triviality of such an enormous
undertaking, I gave the order to my coachman to spur
on my horses, which did some little damage to Prince
Murat's carriage in passing. But, thoroughly worked up
over the Le Moine business, I had already forgotten that

of the carriage, important as it was for what concerns the smooth functioning of the justice and honor of the kingdom, when on the very day of the parvulo at Saint-Cloud, the Ducs de Mortemart and de Chevreuse came to warn me, as one who had at heart the fairest concern for the ancient and indubitable privileges of dukes, the true foundation of the monarchy, that Prince Murat, to whom the royal court had already given the dangerous assurance of its favor, had claimed the royal hand for dinner, claiming precedence over the Duc de Gramont, supporting this fine claim on being the grandson of a man who had been King of the Two Sicilies, as he had explained to M. d'Orléans through Effiat, and had been the chief support of the court of Monsieur his father, so that M. the Duc d'Orléans, utterly embarrassed and moreover not having that clear, clean, profound training whereby a decisive person reduces such whims to nothingness, had not dared to make any definitive decision about this, but had replied that he would see, that he would speak about it with the Duchesse d'Orléans. Strange irony of going off to entrust the most vital interests of the affairs of state, which rests on the privileges of dukes so long as they are not interfered with, to a person who was connected with them only by the most shameful ties and had never known what was proper to herself, much less to Monsieur her husband and to the entire peerage. This very curious and unprecedented reply had been relayed by Princess Soutzo to Messieurs de Mortemart and de Chevreuse who, surprised to the extreme, had immediately come to find me. It is common enough knowledge that she is the only woman who, for my unhappiness, had succeeded in making me emerge from the retirement in which I had been dwelling since the death of the Dauphin and the Dauphine. One scarcely knows oneself the reason for these kinds of preferences, and I could not say how she succeeded, where so many others had failed. She looked like Minerva, as she is represented in the beautiful miniatures on the pendant earrings my mother left me. Her charms had captivated me and I hardly ever stirred from my room in Versailles except to go see her. But I will wait for another part of these Memoirs that will be especially devoted to the Comtesse de Chevigné, to speak at greater length about her and her husband, who had greatly distinguished himself by his valor and was one of the most honest people I have ever known. I had had almost no commerce with M. de Mortemart since the bold cabal he had initiated against me at the Duchesse de Beauvilliers' to make me lose the King's esteem. Never was there a duller mind, one more inclined to be contrary, more tempted to strengthen this contrariness with gibes without any foundation whatsoever, gibes that he then went on to peddle by himself. As for M. de Chevreuse, companion to Monsieur, he was another kind of man and he has been too often spoken of elsewhere here for me to have to go back over his infinite qualities, his science, his kindness, his gentleness, his word that was always kept. But he was a man who, as they say, made mountains out of molehills, a man to dig holes in the moon. We have seen the hours I spent trying to show him the flimsiness of his fantasy about the antiquity of Chevreuse and the fits of rage he almost displayed to the chancellor for building Chaulnes. But in the end, they were both dukes, and very justly attached to the prerogatives of their rank; and since they knew that I myself was more punctilious about ducal prerogatives than anyone at court, they had come to find me because I was moreover a special friend of M. the Duc d'Orléans, and had never had in mind anything but the good of this prince, and had never abandoned him when the intrigues of La Maintenon and the Maréchal de Villeroy left him alone in the Palais Royal. I tried to reason with M. the Duc d'Orléans, I represented to him the insult he was showing not only to dukes, who would all feel wounded in the person of the Duc de Gramont, but to common sense, by letting Prince Murat, like the Ducs de la Tremoïlle earlier, under the empty pretext of being a foreign prince and because his grandfather, so well-known for his bravura, was King of Naples for a few years, take during the parvulo at Saint-Cloud the hand he would make a point not to demand later on at Versailles, at Marly, and that it would serve as a vehicle to being called Highness, since we know where these ridiculous and base ways of princery lead when they are not nipped in the bud. We have seen the effect of this in Messieurs de Turenne and de Vendôme. More authority and a more extensive knowledge were necessary than M. the Duc d'Orléans possessed. Never however was a case simpler, clearer, or easier to explain, more impossible, more abominable to contradict. On one hand, a man who cannot go back more than two generations without getting lost in a night where nothing of note appears; on the other, the head of an illustrious family known for a thousand years, father and son of two Marshals of France, never having admitted any but the greatest alliances. The Le Moine affair itself did not involve interests so vital for France.

During the same period of time, Delaire married a Rohan and rather oddly took the name of Comte de Cambacérès. The Marquis d'Albuféra, who was a good friend of mine as was his mother, filed a number of complaints that, despite the minuscule and, as we will see later on, well-deserved esteem the King had for him, remained without effect. So now he is one of those fine Comtes de Cambacérès (not to mention the Vicomte Vigier, whom we imagine still back in Les Bains where he arose), like the counts de Montgomery and de Brye, whom ignorant Frenchmen think of as descended from G. de Montgomery, so famous for his duel under Henri II, and as belonging to the de Briey family, which included my friend the Comtesse de Briey, who has often figured in these Memoirs and who jokingly called the new Comtes de Brye, who at least were gentlemen of good stock although of lower lineage, *les non brils*.[6]

Another, greater marriage delayed the arrival of the King of England, one that concerned more than just this country. Mlle Asquith, who was probably the most intelligent of anyone, and was like one of those beautiful figures painted in fresco that one sees in Italy,

---

6 A play on *nombril*, "navel," which sounds like "non-Briey." —Trans.

married Prince Antoine Bibesco, who had been the idol of the people who lived where he resided. He was a good friend of Morand, envoy from the King to their Catholic Majesties; he will often be discussed in the course of these Memoirs, as a good friend of my own. This marriage made a great stir, and was applauded everywhere. A few poorly educated Englishmen alas believed that Mlle Asquith was not contracting a good enough marriage. She could indeed lay claim to anything, but they did not know that these Bibescos are related to the Noailles, the Montesquious, the Chimays, and the Bauffremonts who are of Capetian stock and could with great reason claim the crown of France, as I have often said.

Not a single duke, or any titled gentleman, went to that parvulo at Saint-Cloud, aside from me, who came because Mme de Saint-Simon was lady-in-waiting to Mme the Duchesse de Bourgogne, and consented under sheer compulsion, and at risk for any refusal, and out of necessity to obey the King, but with all the suffering and tears we have seen and the endless entreaties of M. the Duc and Mme the Duchesse d'Orléans; the Ducs de Villeroy and de La Rochefoucauld, present because they were unable to console themselves at counting for so little, one might even say for nothing, and wanting to cook up one last little stew of rumors, who used this as an occasion to pay court to the Regent; the chancellor too was there, needing advice, of which he got none that day; at times, Artagnan, Captain of the Guard, would come in, to say that the King was served, or a little later, with the fruit, bringing dog biscuits for the pointers; finally when he proclaimed that the music had begun, by which he fervently hoped to win favorable regard, which yet eluded him.

He was of the house of Montesquiou; one of his sisters had been a lady's maid to the Queen, had gotten ahead nicely, and had married the Duc de Gesvres. He had asked his cousin Robert de Montesquiou-Fezensac to come to this parvulo at Saint-Cloud. Who replied, however, with the admirable apothegm that he was descended from the ancient counts of Fezensac, who were known before Philippe-Auguste, and that he did not see why a hundred years—it was Prince Murat he meant—should have precedence over a thousand years. He was the son of T. de Montesquiou who was well-known to my father and about whom I have spoken in another place, and he had a face and demeanor that gave a powerful sense of what he was and where he came from, his body always slim, and that's an understatement, as if tilted backwards; he could bend forward, actually, when the whim took him, with great affability and with bows of all kinds, but returned quite quickly to his natural position which was all pride, hauteur, intransigence not to bend before anyone and not to yield on anything, to the point of walking always straight ahead without bothering about the way, jostling someone without seeming to see him, or if he wanted to annoy someone, showing that he did see him, that he was in his way, with a great crowd always around him of people of high quality and wit to whom he sometimes bowed right and left, but most often left them, as they say, by the wayside, without seeing them, both eyes fixed in front of him, speaking very loudly, and very well, to those of his acquaintance who laughed at all the funny things he said, and with great reason, as I have said, for he was as witty as can be imagined, with graces that were his alone and that all those who approached him tried, often without wanting to, sometimes even without suspecting they were doing so, to copy and assume, but not one person ever managed to succeed, or do anything but let appear in their thoughts, in their discourse, and in the very air almost, his writing and the sound of his voice, both of which were very singular and very beautiful, like a varnish of his that was recognized immediately and that showed by its light and indelible surface that it was just as difficult not to try to imitate him as it was to manage to do so.

He had often at his side a Spaniard by the name of Yturri whom I had known during my ambassadorship in Madrid, as has been related. At a time when everyone else scarcely ever advanced an opinion except to have his merit noticed, he had that quality, very rare actually, of putting all his own merit into making the Count's shine, helping him in his researches, in his dealings with booksellers, even in matters of the table, finding no task too tedious so long as it spared the Count one, his own task being, if one may say so, only to listen and make Montesquiou's statements resound far and wide, just as those disciples did whom the ancient sophists were accustomed to have always with them, as is evident from the writings of Aristotle and the discourses of Plato. This Yturri had kept the fiery manner of his countrymen, who make a fuss over anything at all, for which Montesquiou chid him very often and very amusingly, to the merriment of all and of Yturri himself first of all, who apologized, laughing at the heatedness of his race, yet took care not to do anything about it, since everyone liked him that way. He was an expert in antique objects, of which knowledge many people took advantage to go see him and consult him about them, even in the retirement our two hermits had resorted to, located, as I have said, in Neuilly, close to the house of M. the Duc d'Orléans.

Those whom Montesquiou invited were very few and very select, only the best and the greatest, but not always the same ones, and this was done expressly, since he played very much at being king, offering favors and disgraces to the point of shameful injustice, but all this was supported by such well-known merit, that others overlooked it in him, but some however were invited very faithfully and very regularly, and one was almost always certain of finding them at his house when he hosted an entertainment, like the Duchesse Mme de Clermont-Tonnerre of whom much will be spoken later on, who was the daughter of Gramont, granddaughter of the famous secretary of state, sister of the Duc de Guiche, who was very much inclined, as we have seen, toward mathematics and painting, and Mme Greffulhe, who was a Chimay, of the famous princely house of the counts of Bossut. Their name is Hennin-Liétard and I have already spoken about the Prince de Chimay, on whom the Elector of Bavaria had the Golden Fleece bestowed by Charles II and who became my son-in-law, thanks to the Duchesse Sforze, after the death of his first wife, daughter of the Duc de Nevers. He was no less attached to Mme de Brantes, daughter of Cessac, of whom it has already been spoken quite often and who will return many times in the course of these Memoirs, and to the Duchesses de la Roche-Guyon and de Fezensac. I have spoken enough of these Montesquious, about their amusing fancy of being descended from Pharamond, as if their antiquity were not great enough and well-known enough not to need to scribble fables, and also about the Duc de la Roche-Guyon, eldest son of the Duc de La Rochefoucauld and ward of his two charges, of the strange present he received from M. the Duc d'Orléans, of his nobility at avoiding the trap that the shrewd villainy of the first president of Mesmes set for him and of the marriage of his son with Mlle de Toiras. One also very often saw there Mme de Noailles, wife of the eldest brother of the Duc d'Ayen, today the Duc de Noailles, whose mother is La Ferté. But I will have occasion to speak of her at greater length as the woman of the finest poetic genius her time has seen, who renewed, and one might even say enlarged, the miracle of the famous Mme de Sévigné. Everyone knows that what I say of her is pure fair-mindedness, it being well enough known by everyone what terms I came to with the Duc de Noailles, nephew of the cardinal and husband of Mlle d'Aubigné, niece of Mme de Maintenon, and I have gone on enough in its place about his intrigues against me to the point of making himself along with Canillac an advocate to the state councillors against people of quality, his skill at deceiving his uncle the cardinal, in criticizing the chancellor Daguesseau, in courting Effiat and the Rohans, in lavishly pouring the enormous pecuniary graces of M. the Duc d'Orléans onto the Comte d'Armagnac to have him marry his daughter, after having failed to snare the eldest son of the Duc d'Albret for her. But I have spoken too much of all that to return to it, of his dark schemes concerning Law, and of the matter of the gemstones, and also of the conspiracy of the Duc and Duchesse du Maine. Quite otherwise, and of quite a different breed, was Mathieu de Noailles, who married the woman in question here, and whom her talent has made famous. She was the daughter of Brancovan, reigning prince of Wallachia, which they call there Hospodar, and had as much beauty as genius. Her mother was a Musurus, which is the name of a very noble family, one of the foremost in Greece, made illustrious by numerous and distinguished ambassadorships and by the friendship of one of those Musuruses with the famous Erasmus. Montesquiou had been the first to speak of her verses. Duchesses went often to listen to his own, at Versailles, at Sceaux, at Meudon, and in the past few years women in town have been imitating them by a familiar strategy, and they invite actors over who recite them, with the aim of attracting one of those ladies, many of whom would go to the house of the Great Nobleman rather than abstain from applauding them there. There was always some recitation in his house at Neuilly, and also the concourse of the most famous poets as well as of the most respectable people and the best company, and on his part, to everyone, and in front of the objects of his house, always a flood of discourse, in that language so peculiar to him that I have described, at which everyone continually marveled.

But every coin has its other side. This man of unrivalled qualities, in whom the brilliant and the profound were equally prominent, this man, who could have been called delightful, who could be listened to for hours to the amusement both of others and of himself, since he laughed loudly at what he said as if he were both author and performer, to their benefit, this man had one vice: he was just as thirsty for enemies as he was for friends. Insatiable for the latter, he was relentless for the former, if one can put it that way, since after a few years had gone by, it was the same ones in whom he had lost all interest. He always needed someone to hate, to pursue, to persecute on the pretext of the most trifling remark— thus he was the terror of Versailles, since he did not in the least restrain his voice, which he employed to hurl the most grievous, biting, unjust remarks at whoever was not to his liking, as when he very clearly proclaimed about Diane de Peydan de Brou, esteemed widow of the Marquis de Saint-Paul, that it was just as unfortunate for paganism as it was for Catholicism that she was named after both Diana and Saint Paul. His choice of words always took people by surprise and made them tremble.

Having spent his youth among the highest society, and his maturity among the poets, and having liked both circles equally, he feared no one and lived in a solitude that he made ever more austere by each former friend that he chased away. He was one of the close friends of Mme Straus, daughter and widow respectively of the famous musicians Halévy and Bizet, wife of Emile Straus, lawyer for a major charity; her admirable retorts are remembered by everyone. Her face had kept all its charm and would have been enough even without her intellect to attract all those who crowded round her. She is the one who, once in the Chapel of Versailles where she had her pew, when M. de Noyon whose language was always so affected and unnatural asked her if the music they were listening to didn't strike her as octagonal, replied, "My dear sir, I was just about to say the same thing!"—as if answering someone who had uttered in front of everyone something that came naturally to mind.

One could fill a whole book if one recounted all that has been said by her and that should not be forgotten. Her health had always been delicate. She had taken advantage of this early on to dispense with the Marlys and the Meudons, so went to pay court to the King only very rarely, whereupon she was always received alone and with great consideration. People were astonished by the fruits and mineral waters she made use of all the time, without any liqueurs, or chocolate, and which had drowned her stomach; Fagon had not wanted to acknowledge this since his reputation was already dwindling. He called "charlatans" all those who prescribe remedies or who had not been received into the Faculty of Medecine; because of such notions he drove away a Swiss who could have cured her. In the end, as her stomach had lost the habit for strong food, and her body for sleep and long walks, she turned this fatigue into a distinction. Mme the Duchesse de Bourgogne came to see her and did not want to be shown beyond the first room. She received duchesses sitting down, who came to visit her just the same, since she was such a delight to listen to. Montesquiou never failed to visit her; he was also highly regarded by Mme Standish, his cousin, who came to that parvulo at Saint-Cloud, being the friend of longest standing of any to be admitted, and the one closest to the Queen of England, and most cherished by her; all the women there did not give way to her as should have been the case but was not, thanks to the incredible ignorance of M. the Duc d'Orléans, who thought little of her since her name was Standish, whereas in fact she was the daughter of Escars, of the house of Pérusse, granddaughter of Brissac; she was one of the greatest ladies in the kingdom as well as one of the most beautiful, and had always lived in the choicest society, of which she was the supreme elixir. M. the Duc d'Orléans also did not know that H. Standish was the son of a Noailles, of the branch of the Marquis of Arpajon. M. d'Hinnisdal had to tell him this. So we had at this parvulo the very remarkable scandal of Prince Murat, on a folding chair, next to the King of England. The stir *that* created resounded far beyond

Saint-Cloud. Those who had the good of the State at heart felt its foundations being undermined; the King, so unversed in the reckoning of births and precedence, but understanding the stain inflicted on his crown by the weakness of having destroyed the highest dignity of the kingdom, attacked Comte A. de La Rochefoucauld on this subject in conversation, who was better versed in this history than anyone and who, ordered to reply by his master, who was also his friend, was not afraid to do so in terms that were so clear and so distinct that he was heard by the entire salon, where however a lively game of lans-quenet was being noisily played. He declared that, though much attached to the greatness of his house, he did not believe that this attachment blinded him or made him conceal anything from anyone, when he found that he was—not to say more—as great a lord as Prince Murat; nonetheless he had always given precedence to the Duc de Gramont and would continue to do so. At which the king forbade Prince Murat under any circumstance from taking anything higher than the title of Highness, or crossing the throne room. The only one who could claim this right was Achille Murat, because he owns sovereign prerogatives in Mingrelia, which is a State bordering territories of the Czar. But he was as simple as he was brave, and his mother, so well-known for her writings, whose charming mind he had inherited, had quickly understood that the substantial reality of his situation among those Muscovites was less than in the more-than-princely house that was hers, since she was the daughter of the Duc de Rohan-Chabot.

Prince J. Murat faltered a bit beneath the storm, just long enough to pass this unfortunate strait, but he wasn't any more troubled than that, and we know that now, even to his cousins, lieutenant generals make no difficulty whatsoever, seeing no deep reason to do so, about addressing him as Your Highness and Sire, while the Parliament, when he goes to greet them, sends out its bailiffs with their staffs raised, an honor which Monsieur the Prince had so much trouble achieving, despite being a prince of the blood. Thus everything declines, everything is debased, everything decays as soon as it is born, in a State where the iron cautery isn't applied right away to pretensions so that they cannot grow anew.

The King of England was accompanied by Lord Derby who was enjoying here, as in his own country, much consideration. He did not have at first sight that air of grandeur and reverie that was so striking in B. Lytton, who has since died, or the singular and unforgettable face of Lord Dufferin. But people liked him perhaps even more, by virtue of a sort of kindliness that the French completely lack and by which they are won over. Louvois had wanted him almost despite himself close to the King because of his abilities and his profound knowledge of the affairs of France.

The King of England avoided calling M. the Duc d'Orléans by that title when he talked to him, but wanted him to have an armchair, to which he did not lay claim, but took care to refuse. The princesses of the blood dined in a manner beyond their station by virtue of an indulgence that got talked about a lot but bore no other fruit. The dinner was served by Olivier, first steward of the King. His family name was Dabescat; he was considerate, beloved by everyone, and so well-known at the court of England that many of the noblemen who were accompanying the King saw him with more pleasure than the knights of Saint-Louis recently promoted by the Regent, whose faces were new. He preserved great loyalty to the memory of the late King and went every year to his memorial service at Saint-Denis, where, to the shame of forgetful courtiers, he was almost always alone with me. I have lingered for a moment over him, because by the perfect knowledge he had of his profession, by his kindness, by his connection to the highest people without being over-familiar, or servile, he had not failed to gain in importance at Saint-Cloud and to become a singular character there.

The Regent made the very true remark to Mme Standish that she was not wearing her pearls as other ladies did, but in a way that the Queen of England had imitated. Guiche was there; he had been brought there as if on a leash out of fear of incurring the Regent's displeasure forever, and was not very much at ease being there. He was much happier at the Sorbonne and in the Academies, where he was sought out more than anyone else. But in the end the Regent had reeled him in; he sensed what he owed in respect of birth, if not of person, to the good of the State, perhaps to his own safety; it would have been too conspicuous if he had not come, and since there was no middle ground between disappearing and refusing to come, he came despite himself. At the word "pearls," I sought him out with my eyes. His own, very similar to his mother's, were admirable, with a gaze that, although no one liked amusing himself as much as he did, seemed to pierce through his pupils, as soon as his mind was engaged in some serious subject. We have seen that he was a Gramont, his name Aure, of that illustrious house made important by so many marriages and positions ever since Sanche-Garcie d'Aure and Antoine d'Aure, Vicomte d'Aster, who took the name and arms of Gramont. Armand de Gramont, who is in question here, with all the seriousness the other lacked, recalled the graces of that gallant Comte de Guiche, who had been so extensively welcomed in the early years of the reign of Louis XIV. He towered over all the other dukes, if only by his infinite knowledge and his admirable discoveries. I can truthfully say that I would say the same things even if I had not received so many marks of friendship from him. His wife was worthy of him, which is saying quite a lot. The position of this duke was unique. He was the delight of the court, the hope, with good reason, of scholars, the friend, without servility, of the highest people, the protector of choice for those who were not yet elevated, the close friend infinitely regarded by José Maria Sert, who is one of the foremost painters in Europe for his likenesses of faces and his smart, enduring decoration of buildings. It has been remarked in its place how, abandoning my berlin for some mules when I was returning to Madrid for my embassy, I had gone to admire his works in a church where they are arranged with prodigious art, between the row of altar railings and columns inlaid with the most precious marble. The Duc de Guiche was chatting with Ph. de Caraman-Chimay, uncle of the one who had become my son-in-law. Their name is Riquet and he truly resembled Riquet with the Tufted Hair as he is portrayed in the fairytales. Despite that, his face promised charm and delicacy and kept its promises, according to what his friends have told me. But I was not at all used to him—we had no commerce, so to speak—and I speak in these Memoirs only of things I have been able to know for myself. I led the Duc de Guiche into the private gallery so that no one could hear us: "Well!" I said to him, "Has the Regent spoken to you of Le Moine?" "Yes," he replied smiling, "and for now, despite these cunctations, I think I have persuaded him." Lest our brief conference be noticed, we had drawn very close to the Regent, and Guiche pointed out to me that they were still talking about gemstones, Standish having explained that in a fire all the diamonds of her mother, Mme de Poix, had burned and turned black, because of which peculiarity, very curious in its effects, they had brought them to the cabinet of the King of England where they were preserved: "But if the diamond was blackened by fire, couldn't coal be changed into a diamond?" asked the Regent, turning to Guiche with an embarrassed air, who shrugged his shoulders and looked at me, confounded by this bewitchment of a man he had thought already dissuaded.

We saw for the first time at Saint-Cloud the Comte de Fels, whose family name is Frich, who came to pay court to the King of England. These Frichs, although they came long ago from the dregs of society, are very glorious. It is to one of them that the good lady Cornuel replied, as he was having her admire the livery of one of his lackeys and added that it came to him from his grandfather: "Oh really, Monsieur? I had no idea that Monsieur your grandfather was a lackey." The presence at the parvulo of the Comte de Fels seemed strange to those who can still be surprised; the absence of the Marquis de Castellane surprised them even more. He had worked for more than twenty years, with the success we know, for the rapprochement of France with England where he had made an excellent ambassador, and the instant the King of England came to Saint-Cloud, his name, illustrious in so many respects, was the first one that had come to his mind. We saw at this parvulo another very singular novelty, that of a Prince d'Orléans traveling in France incognito under the very strange name of an Infante of Spain. I expostulated in vain with M. the Duc d'Orléans that, as great as the house from which this prince came was, one could not conceive of calling an Infante of Spain someone who was not so in his own country, where they give that name only to the heir to the crown, as we have seen in the conversation I had with Guelterio during my ambassadorship to Madrid; and more, that it was only a short step from Infante of Spain to simply Infante, and that the former would serve as a shoehorn for the latter. At which M. the Duc d'Orléans protested that one said simply King only for the King of France, that it had been commanded to

M. the Duc de Lorraine, his uncle, not to let himself say King of France, when speaking of the King, or else he would never leave Lorraine, and finally that if one said the Pope, with nothing more, it's because no other name would be needed. I could offer no reply to any of these fine reasonings, but I knew where the Regent's weakness would lead him, and I made free to tell him. We have seen the result of this, and it wasn't long before people said simply Infante. The King of Spain's envoys went to seek him out in Paris and led him to Versailles, where he paid reverence to the King who remained closeted with him for a good hour, then went into the gallery and presented him, where everyone greatly admired his wit. Near the country house of the Prince de Cellamare he visited that of the Comte and Comtesse de Beaumont whither the King of England had already gone. People said with reason that never had husband and wife been so perfectly made for each other, or for them their magnificent and singular home situated on the pathway to the Annonciades, where it seemed to have been waiting for them for a hundred years. He praised the magnificence of the gardens in perfectly chosen and measured terms, and from there went to Saint-Cloud for the parvulo, but made a scandal there by the unbearable pretension of placing his hand on the Regent. The Regent's weakness made the deliberations reach this highly unprecedented compromise that the Regent and the Infante of Spain entered at the same time, through different doors, into the dining room where the dinner was being given. Thus he hoped to hide his hand. He charmed everyone again with his wit, but did not kiss any of the princesses, but only the Queen of England, which surprised everyone greatly. The King was outraged to learn of the claim on the royal hand and that the Regent's weakness had allowed the plot to be hatched. He did not admit the title of Infante and declared that that prince would be received only with his former rank, immediately after the Duc du Maine. The Infante of Spain tried to reach his goal by other ways. They did not succeed in the least. He stopped visiting the King other than through lingering habit, and at that only irregularly. In the end he suffered from weariness and was seen only rarely at Versailles, where his absence made itself strongly felt, and awoke regret that he had not settled there. But this digression on the peculiarity of titles has taken us too far astray from the Le Moine affair.

(To be continued.)

TRANSLATOR'S ACKNOWLEDGMENT

My thanks to Odile Chilton, Thomas Meyer, and Robert Kelly for their help with this translation; and to Mark Cohen above all, who gave me the idea to translate these pastiches in the first place.

THE CONTEMPORARY ART OF THE NOVELLA

OTHER TITLES IN
THE ART OF THE NOVELLA SERIES

BARTLEBY THE SCRIVENER / HERMAN MELVILLE
THE LESSON OF THE MASTER / HENRY JAMES
MY LIFE / ANTON CHEKHOV
THE DEVIL / LEO TOLSTOY
THE TOUCHSTONE / EDITH WHARTON
THE HOUND OF THE BASKERVILLES / ARTHUR CONAN DOYLE
THE DEAD / JAMES JOYCE
FIRST LOVE / IVAN TURGENEV
A SIMPLE HEART / GUSTAVE FLAUBERT
THE MAN WHO WOULD BE KING / RUDYARD KIPLING
MICHAEL KOHLHAAS / HEINRICH VON KLEIST
THE BEACH OF FALESÁ / ROBERT LOUIS STEVENSON
THE HORLA / GUY DE MAUPASSANT
THE ETERNAL HUSBAND / FYODOR DOSTOEVSKY
THE MAN THAT CORRUPTED HADLEYBURG / MARK TWAIN
THE LIFTED VEIL / GEORGE ELIOT
THE GIRL WITH THE GOLDEN EYES / HONORÉ DE BALZAC
A SLEEP AND A FORGETTING / WILLIAM DEAN HOWELLS
BENITO CERENO / HERMAN MELVILLE
MATHILDA / MARY SHELLEY
STEMPENYU: A JEWISH ROMANCE / SHOLEM ALEICHEM
FREYA OF THE SEVEN ISLES / JOSEPH CONRAD
HOW THE TWO IVANS QUARRELLED / NIKOLAI GOGOL
MAY DAY / F. SCOTT FITZGERALD
RASSELAS, PRINCE OF ABYSSINIA / SAMUEL JOHNSON
THE DIALOGUE OF THE DOGS / MIGUEL DE CERVANTES
THE LEMOINE AFFAIR / MARCEL PROUST
THE COXON FUND / HENRY JAMES
THE DEATH OF IVAN ILYCH / LEO TOLSTOY

THE ART OF THE NOVELLA